THE
CAMEL
EXPRESS

THE
CAMEL
EXPRESS

It really
happened!

BY ANN SHAFFER

ILLUSTRATED BY
ROBIN COLE

GEMSTONE BOOKS

Dillon Press, Inc. Minneapolis, Minnesota 55415

Library of Congress Cataloging-in-Publication Data

Shaffer, Ann.
The camel express / by Ann Shaffer.
(It really happened!)
Summary: As part of an experiment in 1860, a camel fills in for
a wounded pony on a Pony Express route.
ISBN 0-87518-400-6

[1. Pony express—Fiction. 2. Camels—Fiction. 3. West
(U.S.)—Fiction.] I. Cole, Robin, ill. II. Title. III. Series.
PZ7.S52767Cam   1989
[Fic]—dc 19   88-20268
                                                          CIP
                                                          AC

Dillon Press, Inc., 242 Portland Avenue South
Minneapolis, Minnesota 55415

Printed in the United States of America
1 2 3 4 5 6 7 8 9 10 98 97 96 95 94 93 92 91 90 89

TO MOM AND DAD, DAVID AND ANGELA,
AMY AND MARY PAT, SAMANTHA AND TABATHA

CONTENTS

CHAPTER

O N E

THE MOST AMAZING ANIMAL

Mary Claire McCoy lived on a homestead on the grassy plains of the Nebraska Territory just outside of the town of Scotts Bluff, with her mama and her papa, and her Grandpa McCoy. Mary Claire enjoyed life on the farm. She liked wandering in the tall prairie grass, chasing after butterflies, and playing on the banks of the North Platte River. And whenever the pony express rider came whizzing by with his saddle-

9

bags full of mail, she liked to run out by the trail, waving her arms and shouting "Howdy!" to him as he passed. But more than anything else, Mary Claire liked being with her grandpa.

Mary Claire and her grandpa were very good friends. She followed him around the farm, talking to him whenever she had time between school and her chores. Grandpa told her amazing stories about hunting bears in the Rocky Mountains, and alligators in Florida swamps. He had traveled all over North America when he was young, living a life of adventure, so he had many exciting stories to tell.

What Mary Claire liked best about

her grandpa was that she never knew what he would do next. Once he blew a hole in the barn roof trying to make purple fireworks for the Fourth of July. Another time he almost lost a finger to a coyote he was trying to tame. But nothing he had ever done prepared Mary Claire for what she saw one day when she came home from school.

Standing out in front of the house, tied to a fence post, was the most amazing animal Mary Claire had ever seen. What in the world could it be? It had four legs, like a horse or a cow, but it was much, much taller than most four-legged creatures, and it had a great big hump on its back. Though it stood there quietly munching on hay, Mary Claire was afraid to get very close.

"Well, what do you think, Mary Claire?" shouted Grandpa as he strolled out of the house all excited and smiling. "It's a camel! I found him this morning down by the river. Just imagine, he came all the way from the Sahara Desert in Africa!"

At first Mary Claire was speechless. She'd never seen such a thing in her whole life. But when she saw the camel stretch out his neck to nibble on Grandpa's hat, she laughed and came running up to have a closer look.

Pew! The camel smelled terrible! But he had very long eyelashes, and the expression on his face looked just like a smile. Mary Claire was sure the camel was happy to be there. "What's his name, Grandpa?" she asked, shyly petting the animal's side.

"Well, I think we'll call him Carlos. Carlos the camel," said Grandpa proudly.

Just then Carlos succeeded in pushing off Grandpa's hat with his muzzle. He stuck out his big slurpy tongue, and started licking Grandpa's bald head like a horse licking a block of salt.

"Whooee!" yelled Grandpa. "Now you just cut that out!"

But both he and Mary Claire had to laugh when Carlos turned to look at them with his big calm eyes and his funny camel smile. They knew he was just being friendly, in a camel sort of way.

CARLOS SETTLES IN

At supper that evening, Papa told Mary Claire and her mama and Grandpa what he'd been able to find out about Carlos that afternoon in town.

"As far as I can tell," he explained, "Carlos must belong to the United States Army."

"The army!" Mama exclaimed. "What would the army want with such a strange animal?"

"Well, a few years ago they brought

a whole herd of camels over from Africa to use as pack animals," said Papa.

"That's a good idea," Mary Claire commented. "If a camel can walk all over the Sahara Desert, he certainly wouldn't have any trouble getting around here!"

Papa nodded his head. "That's right, Mary Claire. That's exactly what they were thinking."

"So did the army leave poor Carlos behind?" asked Mary Claire.

"I'm sure they didn't leave him behind on purpose," said Papa. "Carlos probably just wandered away from the herd. But I left a message in Burn's General Store, so they'll know where

to find him. In the meantime, I guess we've got ourselves a camel!"

In just a few days Carlos was settled comfortably into life on the farm. At first the horses and other animals were terrified of him. Just the smell of the camel made them try to run away. But after a while they got used to Carlos. Grandpa put him to work hauling firewood from the creek bed.

Every afternoon Carlos would kneel down so Grandpa could climb up on his hump. Then Carlos would take off across the plain, faster than any horse could run. Grandpa held on tight to the reins, laughing and yelling "Whooee! Whooee!" as they sped out of sight.

When they came back, Carlos would kneel down again so Mary Claire could climb up for a ride. As Grandpa led Carlos down to the river and back, Mary Claire liked to pretend she was an Arabian princess riding across the desert to meet her prince.

CHAPTER

T H R E E

PONY EXPRESS
IN DISTRESS

After all the uproar about finding a
camel died down, life went on as usual
for Mary Claire and her family. But just
when Mary Claire began to think nothing exciting would ever happen to her
again, something exciting did happen,
more exciting than anything she could
ever imagine.

One evening, after dinner, Mary
Claire set off to the river to fetch some
water. Before she'd gone far, she heard

hoofbeats in the distance. It sounded like the pony express rider, so Mary Claire decided to stand next to the trail and wait for him to pass by. But just as the rider and pony came into sight, the horse reared up on its hind legs and threw the rider. The pony trotted off into the grass, while the rider lay there on the ground without moving.

When Mary Claire yelled, Papa and Grandpa came running from the barn. They went to help the rider while Mary Claire tried to catch the pony.

Papa and Grandpa carried the pony express rider into the house, and laid him down on Mary Claire's bed. They were afraid his leg was broken. The rider was a boy named Seth, about sixteen years old. He said something had surprised his pony, and made him rear.

Seth was small, and his clothes were very dusty from the trail. His face was pale because of the pain, but he tried to smile when he spoke. "I'm obliged to you all. You're very kind. But I'm afraid I'll have to get back on my pony and ride."

"Oh, nonsense," cried Mama. "You can't possibly ride with a broken leg!"

"But the mail, ma'am!"

"Don't you worry, young man. These folks will get you a doctor," said Grandpa. "And I'll carry the mail to the next station myself."

The next thing Mary Claire knew, Grandpa was climbing up on top of Carlos, with the mailbag over one arm. She watched him, wishing she could climb up onto the hump, too, as she'd done so many times before. Just then Grandpa glanced back at her and shouted, "What are ya waitin' for? Get on!" Then, once they were both settled, he blew a kiss to the family and shouted, "Okay, boy, let's get moving!"

In seconds, Carlos, Mary Claire, and Grandpa were speeding across the plain, and the warm lamplight of home disappeared into the darkness behind them. At first Grandpa held Carlos back a bit as he tried to let his eyes get used to the darkness. A storm was brewing, so there was no starlight or moonlight. Everything was black and still. But by the time the wind started picking up, Grandpa was able to see a little better, so he let Carlos run at full speed.

"How far do we have to go, Grandpa?" Mary Claire shouted to be heard over the noise of the wind.

Grandpa shouted back, "As near as I can figure, it's about fifteen miles to the next station. We'll be following the river. In fact, in a few miles this trail winds right down into the river valley."

Mary Claire knew what that meant. With all the trees, the river valley was a perfect spot for an ambush. Suddenly,

she felt terribly afraid. Great danger
might be waiting for them behind every
tree! But then Mary Claire remem-
bered that they were riding a camel
that was faster than any horse alive.
Carlos would get them through, even if
a hundred Indian warriors were waiting for them.

As they approached the river valley,
Mary Claire could hear the wind stir-
ring up stronger through the trees.
The storm was going to be a bad one.
Suddenly, flash! A bolt of lightning cut
through the sky. In that instant of
light, Mary Claire thought she saw a
face among the trees. Were Indians waiting for them? She couldn't know for

sure, but they weren't going to turn back now. Grandpa shouted to her to stay low and watch out for tree branches. They both whooped to urge Carlos on. "Whooee, Carlos! Let's fly!"

Soon they were almost through the trees, but just as they rounded the last bend in the trail, Mary Claire saw three men with three glinting guns standing right in their path. Bandits!

Grandpa and Mary Claire didn't know what to do. But before they had a chance to think much about it, Carlos began to pick up speed, running faster and faster toward the bandits. And then, all at once, with a loud camel grunt and groan, Carlos leaped right over the surprised bandits and took off up the trail, out of the river bottom.

"What a camel!" Grandpa and Mary Claire exclaimed together, as they left the bandits far behind.

CHAPTER

F O U R

A RUSHING, SWIRLING FLOOD

Back up on higher ground, Mary Claire felt safer. But just about this time the rain began. It came down in torrents so fast and heavy that she could hardly see. The thunder boomed in the sky, and bolts of lightning struck the few trees that were on the plain. Sitting high up on Carlos's hump, Mary Claire was afraid of getting struck, too. She closed her eyes and held on to Grandpa for dear life.

Finally the rain and lightning began to let up. "We'll be coming to a small stream soon," Grandpa shouted. "Once we're past it, we'll be more than half-way to the pony express station."

But when they came to where the stream should have been, Grandpa and Mary Claire could hardly believe their eyes. The little stream had swollen in-to a rushing, swirling flood!

This time, Mary Claire was sure it was all over. Carlos was a desert ani-mal, he couldn't swim. They'd have to turn back, she told herself. They just couldn't get the mail through.

And at first, it looked like Mary Claire was right. Carlos stopped short,

just at the edge of the water. He carefully put one hoof into it, and then pulled it out.

"Come on, Carlos," Grandpa said, trying to turn him around. "I know you can't swim. That's okay, boy, we did what we could."

But Carlos wasn't about to turn around. He just needed to get used to the water a little, like anyone would, before taking a swim. Before they knew what was happening, Carlos trudged on out into the deep water, and then began to swim easily across.

"Whooee! Where'd you learn how to swim, Carlos? Did they teach you that in the army?"

Carlos made no answer, but just kept swimming. At last, he pulled himself up on the opposite bank, and gave himself a good shake. And then suddenly they were off and running again across the plain at top speed.

CARLOS SAVES THE DAY

Carlos ran and ran. But when they finally got to the next station, the place was deserted. Mary Claire squinted her eyes, trying to see better in the darkness. The door to the main building stood open, swinging in the wind, squeaking eerily in the dark night. The stable door lay smashed into splinters on the ground, and all the ponies were gone.

Grandpa said, "It looks to me like

the men have been chased away by Indians. We'll have to ride another twenty miles to the next station!"

All through that long ride, Carlos proved what a wonder of a camel he was. Then, finally, after ploughing through mud two feet deep, sneaking past an Indian camp, and outrunning a pack of hungry wolves, they arrived at the pony express station.

Just imagine how surprised the station manager was when he saw the three of them. He was expecting a young boy on a pony, but what he saw was an old man and a young girl on a camel! But without a second thought, Grandpa tossed the mailbags to the boy waiting to get on a fresh pony. In an instant the boy sped off with the mail, riding westward to the next station.

"Well, you did a fine job, Carlos, my friend," said Grandpa.

Mary Claire scratched Carlos behind the ears, just where he liked to be scratched, and said, "What a camel! Carlos, you're the best camel in the whole world!"

In return, Carlos gave each of them one of his big slurpy camel licks on the head. Then, since they were all very hungry after their long trip, Carlos wandered off to eat some thistles (camels like thistles, you know) and Mary Claire and Grandpa went on into the station to have some stew with the station manager. Then, after their meal, they both went to sleep a while, before they began their long trip back to the farm. And all night long Mary Claire dreamed about the exciting stories she would tell her mama and papa about her adventures on the Camel Express.

THE PONY EXPRESS

The Pony Express was a mail delivery service that operated before the time of airplanes—even before railroads had developed. From the spring of 1860 to the fall of 1861, young men (mainly lightweight teenagers) on horseback galloped with the mail from Saint Joseph, Missouri, all the way to Sacramento, California. Part of the westward route followed along the Platte River in what is now the state of Nebraska.

The Pony Express had hundreds of fast horses and many riders and mail stations. Each rider rode from forty to fifty miles, changing horses every fifteen minutes or so at one of the stations along the route. By passing the mailbags from one rider to the next, they could deliver the mail two thousand miles in eight days.

The Pony Express finally went out of business. Because of the newly completed cross-continent telegraph line and the soon-to-be-completed cross-continent railroad, the mail relay system was no longer necessary.

THE "U.S. CAMEL CORPS"

In 1856 the United States Army imported about eighty camels from Africa and Asia to use as pack animals in the Southwest. The seven-foot-tall, thousand-pound camels could carry huge loads for long distances—from Texas to California. Unfortunately, the strangeness of the camel, its terrible smell, its habit of spitting, and its frightening groans and growls caused many of its American caretakers to dislike camels very much. As a result, the army personnel often mistreated them and the camels became stubborn and mean. An angry camel is very dangerous, capable of trampling people and biting their hands off.

As the army began to realize its experiment had failed, the railroad system was developing rapidly. Soon, fast-moving trains replaced the cargo-carrying camels, and the army sold as many camels as it could to private citizens, circuses, and zoos. Those animals not sold were set loose to run free on the plains and in the deserts of the Southwest.